WHISPERS OF THE UNSEEN

MOHITH MOHAN

To my Paru, for all the love and support

To my parents & Friends

Contents

ONE
THE BEGINNING

Kalpana Hegde had always been the pride of her family. Born and brought up in the small coastal town of Udupi, she had grown accustomed to being the perfect daughter, the one who excelled in everything she did. Her parents, strict yet loving, had always pushed her towards excellence. Studies, studies, and more studies—that was the mantra they had instilled in her from a tender age. And Kalpana, ever obedient, had followed it to the letter.

Now, at 20, she was in her third year at HMS College of Technology in Bangalore, one of the most prestigious institutions in the city. It was the kind of college that her parents had dreamed of for her—a place where the brightest minds gathered, and where she had made her mark as one of the top students in her class.

But despite her academic success, there was something about Bangalore that unsettled her. The city was too big, too fast. Unlike the quiet, serene life of Udupi, Bangalore was a whirlwind of activity—noisy, crowded, and, at times, overwhelming. The college was no different. Here, everyone seemed to be running a race, and Kalpana, though ahead of many, often felt like she was struggling to keep up.

Her classroom was a reflection of the city's chaos. The lecturers were strict, the syllabus was heavy, and the competition was cutthroat. But what bothered her most was the group of boys who had made it their mission to turn every class into a scene of disruption.

Six boys—loud, unruly, and brash. They were the sort who seemed to take pride in being the troublemakers. While the rest of the class listened attentively, they would whisper, laugh, and crack jokes, oblivious to the angry glares from

the teachers. Kalpana couldn't stand them. Their very presence irked her.

Among them, Darshan was the worst. He was tall and lean, with a perpetual smirk on his face, as if he found the whole world amusing. His hair was always unkempt, his uniform never properly ironed. He was the kind of boy who seemed to think rules were meant to be broken. And break them he did, with reckless abandon that often landed him in trouble.

Kalpana had never spoken to Darshan directly, nor did she have any desire to. To her, he was everything she despised—undisciplined, irresponsible, and completely unfocused. She couldn't understand why someone like him was even in a college like HMS. It was a place for serious students, not for those who treated it like a playground.

One day, during a particularly monotonous lecture on digital circuits, the class was interrupted by the sound of muffled laughter. Kalpana didn't have to look to know who was responsible. It was the gang of six, huddled together in the back of the room, passing around a piece of paper and snickering like schoolboys.

The lecturer, Mr. Rao, an elderly man with a no-nonsense attitude, paused mid-sentence and fixed them with a steely glare.

"What is so funny back there?" he demanded, his voice cutting through the air like a whip.

The laughter died down, but the boys remained silent, their expressions still mocking.

"Darshan!" Mr. Rao barked. "Stand up!"

Darshan rose lazily from his seat, that infuriating smirk still on his face.

"What's the joke?" Mr. Rao asked, his eyes narrowing.

Darshan shrugged, his nonchalance only fuelling Kalpana's anger. She clenched her fists under the desk, willing Mr. Rao to throw him out of the class.

But Mr. Rao, known for his short temper, didn't bother to entertain the scene any longer. His face flushed with anger, he slammed his books shut and pointed towards the door. "If you all think this is a joke, then you can teach yourselves!" he snapped. Without another word, he stormed out of the classroom, leaving a stunned silence in his wake.

The moment the door clicked shut, the class erupted into murmurs. Some students, seizing the opportunity, quickly gathered their belongings and slipped out of the room, eager to escape the lecture. Others stayed back, curious to see what would happen next.

Kalpana, frustrated at the interruption, buried herself in her notebook, trying to revise the circuit diagrams Mr. Rao had been discussing. But the hum of activity around her made it hard to focus.

The group from the college music club, who had been sitting near the front, suddenly perked up at the unexpected free time. One of them, a boy named Arjun, grinned and nudged his friend. "Looks like we've got time for some practice," he said, pulling out a guitar from under his desk.

A few others from the club followed suit, bringing out their instruments. They quickly formed a small circle in the front of the classroom, strumming and humming tunes as they began their impromptu practice session.

Darshan and his gang, who had been watching the scene unfold, exchanged amused looks. "Looks like the nerds are trying to entertain themselves," one of them jeered, loud enough for everyone to hear.

The music group ignored them at first, focused on tuning their instruments. But as the mocking continued, Arjun finally had enough. He turned to Darshan's group, his eyes narrowing. "If you think it's so funny, why don't you try playing something better?" he challenged.

Darshan's gang hooted in response, but Darshan himself just leaned back in his chair, smirking. "And what if we do?" he asked, his tone light but taunting.

"Then show us what you've got," Arjun shot back, his voice firm. "Prove you're not all talk."

The classroom fell silent again, the air thick with anticipation. Kalpana, despite herself, found her attention drawn to the exchange. She didn't know why, but there was something about the challenge that intrigued her.

Darshan finally stood up, the smirk still plastered on his face. "Alright then," he said, walking over to where Arjun stood with his guitar. "Let's see what you guys are so proud of."

To everyone's surprise, Darshan picked up one of the guitars, handling it with a confidence that immediately silenced his critics. He strummed a few chords, the sound crisp and clear, echoing through the room.

Without any further provocation, Darshan began to play. The tune started off slow, a soft, melodic line that gradually built up in intensity. The others watched in stunned silence as his fingers moved expertly across the strings, the melody weaving through the air like a spell.

And then, as if on cue, Darshan began to sing. His voice was deep and rich, filled with an emotion that caught everyone off guard. It wasn't just a song—it was a story, one that spoke of longing, of dreams unfulfilled, and of a yearning for freedom. The lyrics, though simple, were poignant, and Kalpana found herself unexpectedly moved.

As the song reached its crescendo, Kalpana noticed the shift in the room. The laughter had died, the mockery forgotten. Even Darshan's own friends had fallen silent, their expressions transformed from amusement to admiration.

When the last note finally faded, there was a moment of profound silence, as if no one dared to break the spell that had been cast. And then, slowly, the room erupted into applause. Even the music club members, who had initially challenged him, couldn't help but clap in appreciation.

Darshan looked up, his smirk replaced by something softer, almost contemplative. His gaze flickered across the room, and for the briefest of moments, his eyes met Kalpana's. He gave a small nod, as if acknowledging her presence, before handing the guitar back to Arjun and walking back to his seat.

Kalpana blinked, trying to process what had just happened. This was the same Darshan she had despised? The same boy she had written off as a good-for-nothing troublemaker?

She didn't know what to think. All she knew was that something had shifted within her, something she couldn't quite put into words. And as she watched Darshan return to his group of friends, who were now looking at him with newfound respect, she felt a strange, inexplicable pull towards him.

But she shook it off. This was ridiculous. Darshan was still the same—still irresponsible, still infuriating. Just because he could play the guitar didn't change who he was.

Or did it?

Kalpana didn't have the answer. All she knew was that, for the first time, she found herself looking at Darshan not with disdain, but with a faint, reluctant curiosity.

TWO

THE AFTERMATH

The days following the unexpected music session left Kalpana more unsettled than she cared to admit. She had always prided herself on being focused, especially with exams around the corner. But Darshan's performance in the classroom was a distraction she hadn't anticipated. The way he sang, the passion in his voice—it was as if he had unlocked something within her, something she couldn't quite understand.

Determined not to let it affect her, Kalpana threw herself into her studies. She spent long hours in the library, avoiding the chatter of her classmates and the thoughts that threatened to pull her away from her books. But no matter how hard she tried, she couldn't stop thinking about Darshan—his voice, his music, and the strange connection she had felt when he sang.

She told herself it was nothing, just a fleeting curiosity. But the more she tried to dismiss it, the more it lingered in the back of her mind.

One afternoon, about a week after the incident, Kalpana was seated in the college canteen, reviewing her notes for an upcoming test. The canteen was bustling with the usual activity—students chatting, laughing, and taking a break from the monotony of classes.

As she sipped her chai, a burst of laughter drew her attention to a nearby table. There, as usual, was Darshan with his gang, including Ishan, occupying one of the corners. They were making some poor first-year student the target of their jokes, their loud voices dominating the room.

Kalpana frowned, feeling the familiar irritation rise within her. She hated how they always seemed to take up so much space, their arrogance spilling over into everything they did. But as she watched, she noticed something different this time. Darshan wasn't leading the mockery as he usually did. Instead, he sat back, quieter than usual, a contemplative look on his face.

He seemed distracted, his mind elsewhere. Kalpana observed as he absentmindedly strummed his fingers on the table, as if playing an invisible guitar. It was a small gesture, but it spoke volumes to her. There was something on his mind, something that set him apart from the boisterousness of his friends.

Ishan, noticing his silence, nudged him with an elbow. "Oi, Darshan! You're not getting soft on us, are you?" he teased, a sly grin on his face. "Don't tell me the music club got to you!"

The others chuckled, but Darshan merely smirked and shook his head. "You wish," he replied, his voice low but firm. "Just thinking about something."

Kalpana felt a strange mix of curiosity and unease. What could Darshan possibly be thinking about? It wasn't like him to be so quiet, so introspective. She quickly dismissed the thought, reminding herself that it was none of her business.

But fate, it seemed, had other plans.

Later that evening, after a long study session in the library, Kalpana was on her way back to the hostel. The sun had set, and the campus was bathed in the soft glow of twilight. She walked briskly, eager to get back to her room and rest.

As she rounded a corner near the hostel, she heard the soft strumming of a guitar, the notes floating through the cool evening air. Kalpana paused, her heart skipping a beat. The sound was coming from the open terrace of the ladies' hostel—a place usually reserved for late-night study sessions or quiet conversations among friends.

Curious, Kalpana made her way up to the terrace, her steps slow and cautious. As she reached the top, she was greeted by an unexpected sight: Darshan, sitting on the low wall with his guitar, his fingers moving gracefully over the strings. But he wasn't alone.

Standing next to him, listening intently, was Miss Disha Kapoor, Kalpana's favourite teacher. In her late 20s, Miss Kapoor was known for her kind heart and passion for teaching. She had always been a source of inspiration for Kalpana, someone who balanced warmth with wisdom. Seeing her here, so immersed in Darshan's music, took Kalpana by surprise.

There were no other students around—just Darshan and Miss Kapoor, standing close together in the dim light. The scene was intimate, almost too personal for Kalpana to witness. But she couldn't tear her eyes away.

Darshan began to sing, his voice low and soulful, the melody carrying a deep sense of longing. Miss Kapoor stood by his side, her eyes closed, as if lost in the music. The way she listened, so absorbed and captivated, made Kalpana's heart ache with a feeling she couldn't quite name.

As the song ended, there was a moment of silence. Then, without a word, Miss Kapoor stepped forward and hugged Darshan, a gesture filled with warmth and affection. It was brief, but it spoke volumes.

Kalpana felt a pang of something—was it jealousy? Confusion? She wasn't sure. All she knew was that this moment, this connection between Darshan and Miss Kapoor, was something she hadn't anticipated. It made her see Darshan in a new light, one that both intrigued and unsettled her.

Unable to watch any longer, Kalpana quietly slipped away, her mind swirling with thoughts. As she descended the stairs, she felt a knot in her stomach, a mix of emotions she couldn't untangle. Why did she care so much? Why did it matter what Darshan did, or who he was close to?

That night, as she lay in bed, Kalpana couldn't shake the image of Darshan and Miss Kapoor from her mind. The way they had connected through the music, the way they had shared that moment, made her feel something she hadn't felt before. It was as if her carefully ordered world was beginning to unravel, and she had no idea how to stop it.

Kalpana didn't know where this would lead, but one thing was clear: her life was about to change in ways she could never have imagined.

THREE

UNRAVELLING TRUTHS

The following weeks were a whirlwind of emotions for Kalpana. What she had witnessed on the hostel terrace played over and over in her mind. Miss Disha Kapoor had always been her role model—someone she looked up to for guidance, wisdom, and compassion. Yet, seeing her in such an intimate moment with Darshan, the very boy she had tried so hard to ignore, left Kalpana feeling confused and betrayed.

Kalpana began avoiding Miss Kapoor in class, choosing seats at the back of the room, where she could focus on her notes without making eye contact. But despite her best efforts, she couldn't shake the feelings of curiosity and jealousy that gnawed at her. Why was she so affected by what she saw? And why did it seem like Darshan was always on her mind now?

Meanwhile, Darshan's presence in the classroom became even more unsettling for Kalpana. He continued to joke around with his friends, his carefree attitude unchanged, but every so often, she would catch him glancing her way. Each time their eyes met, Kalpana's heart would race, and she would quickly look away, afraid that he might somehow sense the turmoil he had caused within her.

One afternoon, Kalpana found herself alone in the college library. She had gone there intending to bury herself in her studies, but the silence of the place only amplified her thoughts. She couldn't concentrate, not with the image of Darshan and Miss Kapoor still so fresh in her mind.

Unable to focus, Kalpana decided to take a walk around the campus to clear her head. She needed to sort through her feelings, to make sense of the confusion that had taken hold of her. As she walked, her feet seemed to have a mind of their own, leading her toward the music club room.

The sound of guitar strings being plucked reached her ears as she approached. Without thinking, Kalpana peeked inside the slightly open door. To her surprise, she found Darshan sitting alone, strumming his guitar. The usual group of troublemakers was nowhere in sight. It was just Darshan, lost in his music, with a look of concentration on his face that Kalpana had never seen before.

For a moment, she hesitated, her heart beating loudly in her chest. But before she could decide whether to walk away or step inside, Darshan looked up and caught her watching him. There was no way to hide now.

"You can come in, you know," Darshan said, his voice surprisingly soft and devoid of its usual teasing tone. "I don't bite."

Kalpana stood frozen at the doorway, unsure of what to do. Every instinct told her to leave, to avoid this encounter at all costs. But something in Darshan's eyes held her there, a quiet intensity that made her take a hesitant step forward.

"I didn't mean to interrupt," Kalpana murmured, finally stepping inside the room. She felt awkward, out of place in this space that seemed to belong entirely to Darshan.

"It's okay," Darshan said, putting his guitar down beside him. "I could use a break anyway." He leaned back in his chair, watching her with a curious expression. "So, what brings you here?"

Kalpana shrugged, trying to appear casual. "Just needed to clear my head. I've been studying a lot lately."

Darshan nodded, a small smile playing on his lips. "You're always studying. You should take a break once in a while, you know."

Kalpana looked down, feeling suddenly self-conscious. "I enjoy it. It helps me stay focused."

"Focused on what?" Darshan asked, his tone probing but not unkind. "There's more to life than just academics, Kalpana."

She stiffened at the sound of her name on his lips. He had never spoken to her like this before, and she didn't know how to respond. The familiar annoyance she felt towards him was absent, replaced by a strange sense of vulnerability.

"I know that," Kalpana replied, her voice barely above a whisper. "But it's important to me. My parents expect a lot, and I don't want to disappoint them."

Darshan's gaze softened, and for the first time, Kalpana saw a side of him that she had never noticed before—a side that wasn't the carefree troublemaker she had always dismissed. "It's okay to want to make your parents proud," he said, "but don't lose yourself in the process."

His words struck a chord within her, echoing the very doubts she had been grappling with. Kalpana found herself sitting down on the nearest chair, unable to maintain the emotional distance she had tried so hard to uphold.

"You don't understand," she said, her voice trembling slightly. "My whole life, all I've ever done is study. It's all I know. It's all I'm good at."

Darshan looked at her with a seriousness that belied his usual carefree demeanour. "You're good at more than that, Kalpana. You just haven't given yourself the chance to find out what else you can do."

Kalpana looked up at him, her eyes searching his for any hint of mockery, but there was none. For the first time, she saw Darshan not as a troublemaker or a distraction, but as someone who understood her struggles in a way that no one else did.

They sat in silence for a moment, the tension between them slowly dissolving. It was a strange feeling for Kalpana, this newfound connection with someone she had tried so hard to keep at a distance. She didn't know what to make of it, or what it might mean for her future.

As the minutes ticked by, Kalpana found herself relaxing, the weight of her worries lifting just a little. She was about to say something when the door to the music room creaked open, and Miss Disha Kapoor stepped inside, her eyes widening in surprise at the sight of them together.

"Oh, I didn't realize anyone was here," Miss Kapoor said, her voice laced with hesitation. "I hope I'm not interrupting."

Kalpana quickly stood up, her heart racing. "No, ma'am, we were just... I was just leaving."

Miss Kapoor glanced between them, a flicker of something unreadable passing through her eyes before she smiled warmly. "It's okay, Kalpana. You don't have to leave on my account. I just came to check on the music club's schedule."

But Kalpana was already gathering her things, eager to escape the room before the situation grew more awkward. "I should get back to my studies anyway," she said hurriedly, avoiding Darshan's gaze.

As she made her way to the door, she felt Miss Kapoor's hand on her arm, a gentle touch that stopped her in her tracks. "Kalpana, don't be so hard on yourself," Miss Kapoor said softly. "It's okay to take a break sometimes."

Kalpana nodded, forcing a smile. "Thank you, ma'am. I'll try."

With that, she left the room, her mind a jumble of emotions she couldn't quite process. She felt as though she were standing on the edge of something new, something that both frightened and excited her. And for the first time in a long time, Kalpana wasn't sure what her next step would be.

THE UNSEEN CONNECTION

The days following her encounter with Darshan were a whirlwind for Kalpana. She threw herself into her studies, trying to drown out the confusion swirling in her mind. But no matter how hard she tried, she couldn't shake the image of Darshan in the music room, his gentle words echoing in her ears. She couldn't understand why she was so affected by him—by his presence, his voice, his unexpected depth.

Kalpana's routine became a series of distractions. She woke up early, attended classes, spent hours in the library, and avoided any place where she might run into Darshan. But avoiding him was impossible. His presence seemed to be everywhere—on campus, in her thoughts, and even in her dreams.

One evening, as she sat at her study desk in the hostel, trying to focus on her notes, her mind drifted back to the terrace scene with Miss Disha Kapoor. The way Miss Kapoor had looked at Darshan, the way she had seemed completely absorbed in his singing, left a lingering sense of unease in Kalpana. She had always admired Miss Kapoor's grace and intelligence, but now there was something more—a nagging curiosity mixed with jealousy.

Kalpana's thoughts were interrupted by a knock on her door. It was Meera, her best friend from another batch at HMS College of Technology. Meera was always full of energy, her cheerful nature a sharp contrast to Kalpana's current mood.

"Hey, Kalpana! What's up?" Meera asked as she walked in, dropping her backpack on the floor.

"Nothing much," Kalpana replied, forcing a smile. "Just trying to study."

Meera plopped down on the bed, her eyes narrowing as she studied Kalpana. "You don't look like you're studying. You look like you're thinking too much."

Kalpana sighed, knowing she couldn't hide her feelings from Meera. "It's just... there's been a lot on my mind lately."

"Like what?" Meera asked, genuinely curious.

Kalpana hesitated for a moment, unsure if she should confide in her. But Meera had always been a good listener, and she needed to talk to someone. "It's about Darshan," she finally said.

Meera's eyebrows shot up in surprise. "Darshan? Who's that?"

Kalpana bit her lip, realizing that Meera didn't know anyone from her class. "He's a guy in my class... kind of a troublemaker, but recently, I've started noticing things about him that are... different."

Meera leaned forward, her expression serious. "Like what?"

Kalpana hesitated, then decided to tell Meera about the incident she had witnessed on the terrace. She recounted how she had seen Miss Kapoor and Darshan together, how they had seemed so close, and how it had left her feeling confused and unsettled.

Meera listened carefully, her expression growing more concerned as Kalpana spoke. When she finished, Meera leaned back, her arms crossed. "That's... strange," she finally said. "I mean, Miss Kapoor is one of the most respected teachers here. And this Darshan guy... well, he sounds like trouble."

Kalpana nodded, feeling a mix of relief and anxiety. "I know. That's what's bothering me. I don't understand why I'm so affected by all this. It's like... like there's something I'm missing."

Meera was quiet for a moment, deep in thought. "Maybe you're overthinking it," she suggested. "Or maybe there's more to Darshan than you realize."

Kalpana sighed, rubbing her temples. "I just wish I could figure it out. It's distracting me from everything else."

Meera gave her a reassuring smile. "Maybe you should talk to him. Get to know him better. Maybe that'll help you understand what's going on."

Kalpana looked at her, unsure. "Talk to him? I don't know if I can do that."

"Why not?" Meera asked, her tone encouraging. "What's the worst that could happen? You might actually find out what's going on in that head of his."

Kalpana considered her words, feeling a mix of fear and curiosity. Talking to Darshan seemed like the logical step, but the thought of confronting her feelings was daunting. Still, Meera had a point. She couldn't keep avoiding the issue forever.

"Maybe," she said, though she wasn't entirely convinced.

Meera gave her a reassuring smile. "You'll figure it out, Kalpana. Just don't let it consume you. Remember, you've got exams coming up."

Kalpana nodded, appreciating her concern. "Thanks, Meera. I'll try to focus."

After Meera left, Kalpana sat in silence, her thoughts racing. She knew she couldn't ignore her feelings any longer. Whether she liked it or not, Darshan had become a significant part of her life, and she needed to understand why.

That night, as she lay in bed, sleep eluded her. Kalpana's mind kept returning to the same questions. Who was Darshan, really? Why did he have such a strong effect on her? And what was his connection to Miss Kapoor?

The more she thought about it, the more determined she became. She needed answers. And the only way to get them was to confront Darshan—no matter how difficult it might be.

FIVE

CONFRONTING THE UNKNOWN

Kalpana spent the next few days in a state of restless anticipation. The more she thought about her conversation with Meera, the more she realized that she couldn't continue living in this constant state of confusion. She needed to confront Darshan, to get answers to the questions that were gnawing at her mind. But every time she saw him on campus, her resolve would falter, her nerves getting the better of her.

It wasn't until Friday afternoon that she finally gathered the courage. Kalpana was walking back to her hostel after a particularly draining lecture when she spotted Darshan sitting alone on a bench under the large banyan tree near the college library. He didn't have his guitar with him this time, only his backpack slung over one shoulder as he stared off into the distance, lost in thought.

Taking a deep breath, Kalpana approached him. Her heart pounded in her chest as she rehearsed what she wanted to say, but the moment she was close enough for Darshan to notice her, all her carefully planned words seemed to vanish.

"Hi, Darshan," she said, her voice barely above a whisper.

Darshan looked up, surprised to see her. "Oh, hey Kalpana," he replied, a small smile tugging at the corners of his mouth. "What's up?"

Kalpana hesitated for a moment, her mind racing. But then she reminded herself of why she was here. She needed to know the truth. "Can we talk? There's something I need to ask you."

Darshan's smile faded, replaced by a look of concern. He nodded, gesturing for her to sit down beside him. "Sure, what's on your mind?"

Kalpana sat down, trying to calm her nerves. She glanced at Darshan, who was watching her intently, waiting for her to speak. "It's about the other day... when you were singing on the terrace," she began, her voice trembling slightly. "I saw you with Miss Kapoor."

Darshan's expression remained neutral, but there was a flicker of something in his eyes—something Kalpana couldn't quite decipher. "And?" he asked, his tone cautious.

Kalpana swallowed hard, trying to find the right words. "I... I saw the way she looked at you, the way she was completely immersed in your singing. And then she... hugged you. I just... I don't understand what's going on between you two."

Darshan was silent for a moment, his gaze shifting away from her. When he finally spoke, his voice was quiet, almost contemplative. "Miss Kapoor... Disha... she's someone very special to me. But it's not what you think."

Kalpana frowned, her confusion only deepening. "What do you mean? Are you two... involved?"

Darshan shook his head, a sad smile on his face. "No, it's not like that. Disha has always been there for me, like a mentor. She understands me in ways most people don't. She's helped me through a lot, especially with my music."

Kalpana listened, her mind racing with questions. "But why were you two alone on the terrace? Why did she hug you like that?"

Darshan sighed, running a hand through his hair. "It's complicated, Kalpana. Disha... she's been going through some personal stuff, and that day, she needed someone to talk to. The song I sang—it was something we both connected with. That's why she was so emotional."

Kalpana's heart sank. She had been so quick to jump to conclusions, so consumed by her own emotions, that she hadn't considered the possibility that there might be more to the story. "I'm sorry," she said softly. "I didn't mean to pry. I just... I was confused."

Darshan looked at her, his expression softening. "It's okay. I get it. Things aren't always what they seem, Kalpana. But I appreciate that you came to me to ask instead of making assumptions."

Kalpana felt a wave of relief wash over her. Despite the awkwardness of the conversation, she was glad she had finally confronted Darshan. It had taken a lot of courage, but now that it was done, she felt lighter, as if a weight had been lifted from her shoulders.

As the silence stretched between them, Kalpana found herself feeling more at ease in Darshan's presence. She realized that, despite all the mystery surrounding him, she was drawn to him in a way she hadn't expected. There was something about him that intrigued her, that made her want to know more.

"Can I ask you something else?" Kalpana said, breaking the silence.

Darshan nodded, his eyes meeting hers. "Sure, go ahead."

Kalpana hesitated for a moment before speaking. "Why do you always seem so... distant? Like there's something you're hiding."

Darshan's expression grew serious, and for a moment, Kalpana thought he wouldn't answer. But then he sighed, looking down at his hands. "I guess... I've always been a bit of a loner. I don't let people in easily. There's a lot about me that most people wouldn't understand."

Kalpana studied him, sensing the depth of his words. "You mean your music?"

Darshan nodded slowly. "Yeah, that's part of it. Music is... my escape. It's where I can be myself, without any pretences. But there's more to it than that."

Kalpana leaned in, her curiosity piqued. "Like what?"

Darshan glanced at her, his expression unreadable. "Maybe I'll tell you someday," he said softly. "But for now, let's just say that everyone has their own demons. Mine are just a little more complicated."

Kalpana felt a pang of sympathy for him. She realized that Darshan was carrying burdens she couldn't begin to understand. But instead of feeling frustrated, she felt a growing sense of respect for him. He was more than just the enigmatic troublemaker she had once thought him to be.

As they sat in silence, Kalpana felt a new sense of connection with Darshan. She had come to confront him, but instead, she had found a kindred spirit—someone who, like her, was navigating the complexities of life in his own way.

Finally, Darshan stood up, grabbing his bag. "I should get going," he said, slinging the strap over his shoulder. "But thanks for talking to me, Kalpana. It means a lot."

Kalpana stood up as well, a small smile on her face. "Thank you, too, Darshan. For being honest with me."

Darshan nodded, giving her one last look before turning and walking away. As she watched him disappear into the distance, Kalpana realized that this was just the beginning. There was so much more to discover—about Darshan, about herself, and about the strange connection that seemed to be growing between them.

And for the first time in a long while, Kalpana felt something she hadn't expected—hope.

SIX

THE SHATTERED MIND

Kalpana's thoughts were consumed by Darshan. The memory of their conversation under the banyan tree played over and over in her mind, each replay raising more questions than answers. She had to know more—had to understand the truth about him.

But Darshan had become elusive. He would slip out of class early, avoid common hangouts, and every time she tried to approach him, he seemed to vanish. The mystery gnawed at her, leaving her restless and distracted.

Determined to uncover the truth, Kalpana decided to approach someone who might know him better. She spotted Aditya and the rest of Darshan's gang lounging in the courtyard, laughing and joking as usual. Summoning all her courage, she walked over to them.

"Hey, Aditya," she called out, trying to keep her voice steady.

Aditya looked up, surprised to see her. "Kalpana? What's up? You don't usually hang out with us."

Kalpana forced a smile. "I need to talk to you... about Darshan."

At the mention of Darshan, the boys exchanged confused glances. Aditya raised an eyebrow. "Darshan? Who's that?"

Kalpana felt a chill run down her spine. "Darshan... your friend. The one who's always with you guys."

Aditya frowned, then burst out laughing, nudging the others. "You hear that? She's talking about some imaginary friend!"

Another boy chimed in, "Kalpana, you've been hitting the books too hard. There's no sixth member in our gang. You sure you're not losing it?"

The group erupted into laughter, mocking her with exaggerated gestures and snide remarks. Kalpana's heart sank. This wasn't the reaction she had expected. Their laughter echoed in her ears, turning into a harsh, unforgiving noise that filled her with dread.

"But... I've seen him. I've talked to him," she insisted, her voice trembling.

Aditya shook his head, still chuckling. "Kalpana, there's no Darshan. You're imagining things. Better take a break before you really go mad."

Their laughter continued as Kalpana turned and walked away, her world crumbling around her. Every step felt heavy, every breath suffocating. How could they not know him? How could they not see what she saw?

Days passed, and Kalpana found herself unable to leave her hostel room. The once vibrant and determined girl was now a shadow of her former self. She stopped attending classes, withdrew from her friends, and spent her days in bed, staring blankly at the ceiling.

Her emotional state was shattered. The truth—or what seemed like the truth—was too much for her to bear. She kept replaying the conversations in her mind, desperate to find some clue, some sign that Darshan was real. But with each passing day, that hope faded, leaving behind only confusion and despair.

One evening, Miss Disha Kapoor knocked on her door. Kalpana's heart leapt at the sight of her favourite teacher, a glimmer of hope sparking in her chest.

"Miss Disha, please, you have to tell me," Kalpana pleaded, her voice hoarse from days of crying. "Darshan... where is he? I know he's real, I know I didn't imagine him."

Miss Disha looked at her with deep concern, her usual calm demeanour replaced by worry. She stepped inside and sat on the edge of Kalpana's bed, taking her hand gently.

"Kalpana," she began softly, "I don't know who you're talking about. There is no student named Darshan in our college. I've checked the records myself."

Kalpana shook her head violently, tears streaming down her face. "No, that's not true! I saw you with him, Miss! You were on the terrace, and he was singing to you. You hugged him... you know him!"

Miss Disha's expression softened with sorrow. "Kalpana, I don't remember anything like that. I'm worried about you. I think you've been under too much stress."

Kalpana clung to Miss Disha's hand, her grip tightening as she begged, "Please, tell me the truth! He's real, he has to be real..."

But Miss Disha could see the pain in Kalpana's eyes, the desperation in her voice. Realizing that this was beyond anything she could handle alone, she decided to take action.

"I'm going to call your parents, Kalpana," Miss Disha said gently, trying to keep her voice calm. "You need to go home and rest. They'll take care of you."

"No, no, you can't," Kalpana protested, but her voice was weak, her resolve crumbling.

Miss Disha squeezed her hand reassuringly. "It's going to be okay, Kalpana. We'll get through this together."

Kalpana didn't have the strength to argue anymore. She nodded weakly, tears still flowing down her cheeks. Miss Disha stayed with her until her parents arrived later that evening. They were distraught at the sight of their daughter, their once-bright Kalpana now so lost and broken.

With great care, they helped her pack a few things and gently guided her out of the hostel. Kalpana glanced back at the room she was leaving behind, the place where she had spent so many sleepless nights, haunted by the phantom of Darshan.

As they drove away from the college, Kalpana's heart felt heavy with a mixture of sorrow and confusion. The world outside the car windows blurred, her mind too exhausted to make sense of anything anymore. All she could do was lean on her parents and hope that, somehow, she would find the strength to heal.

SEVEN
A New Beginning

A few years had passed since the tumultuous events at HMS College, but the memories still lingered in the corners of Kalpana's mind. After taking time off to recover, she eventually completed her graduation from a local university, determined not to let her past define her future. Now, she was pursuing an MBA in Business Analytics at St. Teresa College in Goa, a new chapter in her life that promised a fresh start.

St. Teresa College was a world apart from HMS. Nestled near the serene beaches of Goa, the campus had a laid-back vibe that Kalpana found comforting. The palm trees swayed gently in the breeze, and the distant sound of waves crashing against the shore provided a soothing backdrop to her studies. It was the perfect place for someone looking to rebuild themselves, to move past the shadows of their past.

Kalpana had thrown herself into her studies with a single-minded focus, determined to excel in her course. She had learned to compartmentalize her emotions, locking away the memories of Darshan and the confusion that had once consumed her. But despite her best efforts, there were times when those memories would surface, unbidden and unwelcome, like ghosts from a life she had tried to leave behind.

One evening, after a particularly intense day of classes, Kalpana returned to her hostel room, her mind heavy with thoughts of the upcoming exams. The pressure was building, as it always did before an important test. She had spent hours poring over her notes, trying to cram as much information as possible. The anxiety gnawed at her, making it hard to concentrate, and she could feel the familiar tension creeping in.

She knew she needed a break, something to take her mind off the exams, if only for a little while. But the thought of relaxing made her feel guilty—there was so much more she could be studying. Her parents had always stressed the importance of education, pushing her to be the best, and those expectations weighed heavily on her even now.

As she sat at her desk, staring blankly at her textbooks, her phone buzzed in her pocket. It was a message from Meera, her best friend and confidante, who had been a constant source of support since the events at HMS.

"Hey Kalps, there's a shack near Anjuna Beach that has live music tonight. Wanna join?"

Kalpana hesitated, her mind still on her exams. She had told herself she would spend the entire evening studying, but she could feel the pressure mounting, the same kind of pressure that had once driven her to the brink. Maybe a short break wouldn't hurt. Maybe it was what she needed to clear her head before diving back into her studies.

"Sure, I'll meet you there," she replied, her fingers trembling slightly as she typed out the message.

Later that evening, Kalpana made her way to the shack. The place was buzzing with energy, filled with tourists and locals alike, all gathered to enjoy the music and the cool evening breeze. Meera was waiting for her near the entrance, waving enthusiastically when she spotted her.

"There you are! You'll love this place," Meera said, giving Kalpana a quick hug.

Kalpana smiled, though she felt a slight unease settling in her chest. "It's been a while since I've been to something like this."

"Don't worry, we'll just relax and have a good time," Meera reassured her, leading her towards a table near the stage.

The evening progressed pleasantly, with laughter, conversation, and the lively music filling the air. For a while, Kalpana managed to push her concerns to the back of her mind, enjoying the moment with Meera. But as the night wore on, and the shack filled with more people, she couldn't shake the feeling that something was about to happen.

And then, it did.

As the band took a break, a solo performer took the stage, a young man with tousled hair and a guitar slung over his shoulder. The moment Kalpana saw him, her heart skipped a beat. He looked familiar—too familiar. But it couldn't be, could it?

He adjusted the microphone, strummed a few chords, and then began to sing. The voice that filled the shack was hauntingly familiar, rich and melodic, sending shivers down Kalpana's spine. She knew that voice. She had heard it before, late at night on a terrace, in another lifetime.

Her breath caught in her throat as the memories came rushing back, the illusion she had carefully built over the years crumbling in an instant. It was Darshan—no, it couldn't be. But the voice, the way he held the guitar, everything about him was the same.

Kalpana stared at him, her mind spinning. Was this another illusion? Another figment of her imagination? She felt light-headed, the room spinning as the weight of the past threatened to overwhelm her.

"Kalps, are you okay?" Meera's voice cut through the fog, filled with concern.

Kalpana barely heard her. All she could do was watch as the man on stage continued to sing, his eyes closed, lost in the music. She felt an inexplicable pull, a connection that she had tried so hard to sever but had never truly succeeded.

When the song ended, the audience erupted in applause, but Kalpana was frozen in place, unable to tear her eyes away from him. The performer opened his eyes, glanced over the crowd, and for a brief moment, their eyes met.

It was as if time had stopped. Kalpana felt a jolt, like electricity coursing through her veins. He looked right at her; his expression unreadable. But there was something in his eyes, something that made her heart pound in her chest. Could it really be him? Could it be Darshan?

But just as quickly, the moment passed. The performer looked away, acknowledging the applause with a nod, and then stepped off the stage, disappearing into the crowd.

Kalpana felt a surge of panic. She had to know. She had to find out who he was. Ignoring Meera's concerned questions, she pushed her way through the crowd, trying to catch up to him. But the shack was packed, and by the time she reached the spot where he had been, he was gone.

She searched frantically, her eyes darting around the room, but there was no sign of him. It was as if he had vanished into thin air.

"Kalpana, what's going on?" Meera caught up to her, grabbing her arm. "You're scaring me. What happened?"

Kalpana shook her head, still in a daze. "I… I thought I saw someone. Someone I knew."

Meera looked at her with concern. "Are you sure you're, okay? Maybe we should go."

Kalpana nodded weakly, the shock of the encounter still reverberating through her. "Yeah, let's go. I think I need some air."

As they left the shack, Kalpana couldn't help but glance back one last time, hoping to catch a glimpse of him. But the crowd had swallowed him up, leaving her with more questions than answers.

As they walked back to the hostel, Kalpana's mind was in turmoil. Could it have really been him? Or was this just another figment of her imagination, a remnant of the past that refused to let her go?

But deep down, she knew that the encounter had reignited something within her, something she had tried to bury for years. The past was not done with her yet, and the truth, whatever it was, was still out there, waiting to be uncovered.

EIGHT

ECHOES OF A NEW DAWN

The days following her encounter with the mysterious singer were a blur for Kalpana. Her mind was a whirlwind of emotions, the line between reality and memory blurring once again. She tried to focus on her studies, pushing herself harder than ever, but the thoughts of that night kept creeping in, distracting her from the path she had so carefully laid out.

Every time she closed her eyes, she could hear that voice—the haunting melody that had once belonged to Darshan. But it wasn't Darshan, it couldn't be. Kalpana knew she had to get to the bottom of this, to find out who the singer was and why his voice had such a powerful effect on her.

One morning, after a restless night spent tossing and turning, Kalpana decided to take a walk along the beach. The gentle sound of the waves and the soft, cool sand beneath her feet had always been a source of comfort. It was a quiet time of day, with only a few early risers out for their morning jogs or yoga sessions. The sun had just begun to rise, casting a warm, golden glow over the water.

As she walked, lost in thought, Kalpana noticed a figure in the distance. A young man, sitting on a rock near the edge of the beach, strumming a guitar. His back was to her, but there was something familiar about the way he held the instrument, the ease with which his fingers moved over the strings.

Kalpana's heart skipped a beat. Could it be him? The singer from the shack?

She approached slowly, not wanting to startle him. As she got closer, the melody became clearer, and she felt a wave of nostalgia wash over her. It was the same haunting tune she had heard that night, the one that had stirred memories she had tried so hard to bury.

The young man looked up as she neared, his eyes meeting hers. There was a moment of recognition, a brief flicker of surprise in his gaze, but it quickly gave way to a warm, easy smile.

"Hey there," he said, his voice as smooth and melodic as his music. "I saw you the other night at the shack, didn't I?"

Kalpana nodded, her heart pounding in her chest. "Yes, I was there. You were... incredible."

"Thanks," he replied, setting his guitar down and standing up. He extended a hand. "I'm Rahul, by the way. And you are?"

"Kalpana," she said, shaking his hand, her voice barely above a whisper. "Kalpana Hegde."

"Nice to meet you, Kalpana." Rahul's smile widened, and there was a twinkle in his eye that reminded her so much of Darshan. It was unsettling, yet at the same time, she felt drawn to him, as if some invisible thread connected them.

For a moment, they stood there in silence, the sound of the waves filling the space between them. Kalpana's mind was racing, torn between the present and the past. She wanted to ask him if he knew Darshan, if there was some connection she was missing, but the words caught in her throat.

"Do you come here often?" Rahul asked, breaking the silence.

"Sometimes," Kalpana replied, trying to steady her voice. "It's a good place to think."

"Yeah, I know what you mean." Rahul looked out at the ocean, a pensive expression on his face. "I come here to clear my head too, especially when I'm working on new music. There's something about the sea that's just... inspiring, you know?"

Kalpana nodded, her eyes fixed on him. There was something about Rahul that put her at ease, despite the turmoil brewing inside her. He was different from Darshan, and yet, there was a similarity that she couldn't quite put her finger on.

They spent the next hour walking along the beach, talking about everything and nothing. Rahul told her about his passion for music, how he had been playing guitar since he was a kid, and how he dreamed of making it big one day. He was a local guy, born and raised in Goa, with a deep love for the place and its vibrant culture.

As they talked, Kalpana found herself opening up to him in ways she hadn't with anyone else since the incident at HMS. There was a comfort in his presence, a feeling of safety that she hadn't felt in a long time. But with every word, every shared glance, the memories of Darshan lingered in the back of her mind, like a shadow she couldn't shake.

The more she got to know Rahul, the more she felt a spark of attachment forming between them. He was kind, funny, and genuinely interested in her, asking about her life, her studies, and her dreams. There was an ease to their conversation that made Kalpana forget, if only for a moment, the pain she had carried with her for so long.

But every time Rahul picked up his guitar, every time he sang, Kalpana was transported back to that terrace, to the night she had first heard Darshan sing. The line between the two men blurred in her mind, leaving her confused and conflicted.

As they reached the end of their walk, Rahul turned to her with a smile. "This was nice, Kalpana. I hope we can do this again sometime."

Kalpana smiled back, though her heart was heavy with the weight of her memories. "I'd like that."

They exchanged numbers, and as Kalpana watched him walk away, she felt a strange mix of emotions—hope, fear, and a lingering sadness that she couldn't quite explain. Rahul was real, flesh and blood, not a figment of her imagination. But the memories of Darshan, of everything she had been through, still haunted her, casting a shadow over this new connection.

As Kalpana made her way back to the hostel, she couldn't stop thinking about Rahul. There was something about him, something that made her want to know more, to explore the possibility of a future with him. But at the same time, she was terrified of what that might mean—of reopening old wounds that had never fully healed.

Could she really let herself be happy again? Could she allow herself to feel something for someone new, when the past still held such a tight grip on her heart?

Only time would tell.

But for now, Kalpana knew one thing: she wasn't ready to give up. She had come too far, fought too hard to rebuild her life. And maybe, just maybe, Rahul was the key to moving forward, to finally letting go of the ghosts that had haunted her for so long.

As she walked back to her room, the sun now fully risen, Kalpana felt a small glimmer of hope. It was faint, barely more than a whisper, but it was there—a sign that, perhaps, there was a future waiting for her, one where she could finally find peace.

NINE

SHADOWS IN THE MUSIC

The days following her encounter with Rahul were filled with a strange mix of anticipation and unease for Kalpana. She was drawn to him in ways she couldn't quite explain, yet every time they spoke or met, memories of Darshan would resurface, casting a shadow over their interactions. It was as if Rahul was the embodiment of everything she had lost and everything she feared to confront again.

Kalpana buried herself in her studies, determined not to let her emotions derail her once more. The exams were just around the corner, and she knew she couldn't afford any distractions. But the harder she tried to focus, the more her mind wandered back to Rahul and the unsettling connection she felt with him.

One evening, after a particularly gruelling study session, Kalpana decided to take a break and visit the beach again. The soothing sound of the waves had become her sanctuary, a place where she could think clearly, away from the chaos of her thoughts.

As she walked along the shoreline, her phone buzzed in her pocket. It was a message from Rahul.

Hey, I'm at the beach. Wanna join me?

Kalpana hesitated. She knew she should be studying, but the pull of the ocean—and Rahul—was too strong to resist. After a moment of indecision, she texted back.

On my way.

When she arrived, she found Rahul sitting on the same rock where she had first seen him, his guitar resting beside him. But this time, he wasn't playing. Instead, he was staring out at the horizon, lost in thought.

"Hey," Kalpana called out softly as she approached.

Rahul turned and smiled, but there was a hint of something else in his eyes—something she couldn't quite place.

"Hey, Kalpana. Glad you could make it," he said, patting the spot next to him.

She sat down, the cool breeze ruffling her hair. "You're not playing tonight?"

Rahul shook his head. "Not tonight. Just thinking."

"About what?"

He paused, as if weighing his words. "About life, music, the future. You ever feel like you're chasing something you can't quite catch?"

Kalpana's heart skipped a beat. "All the time."

Rahul nodded; his gaze still fixed on the horizon. "Sometimes I wonder if I'm chasing the right things. If the dreams I have are really what I want, or just something I've convinced myself I want."

His words hit close to home for Kalpana. She had spent so much of her life pursuing goals that others had set for her—being the top student, getting into the best colleges, making her parents proud. But deep down, she wasn't sure if those dreams were really hers, or if they had been imposed on her by others.

"I know what you mean," she said quietly. "Sometimes, I feel like I'm living someone else's life, like I'm not in control of what happens."

Rahul finally looked at her, his eyes searching hers. "Then maybe it's time to take control. To figure out what you really want and go after it."

Kalpana felt a shiver run down her spine. She wanted to believe it was that simple, but the shadows of her past were always there, lurking just beneath the surface. "It's not that easy," she whispered.

Rahul reached out and gently took her hand, his touch warm and reassuring. "I know it's not. But maybe... maybe it doesn't have to be so hard either."

For a moment, they sat in silence, the only sound the rhythmic crashing of the waves. Kalpana felt a strange sense of peace, as if the turmoil inside her was finally starting to settle.

But just as she began to relax, a familiar tune began to drift through the air. It was coming from a nearby shack, where a group of musicians had gathered to play. The melody was hauntingly beautiful, and Kalpana's heart clenched as she recognized it.

It was the same song Darshan had sung on that fateful night.

Without realizing it, Kalpana's hand tightened around Rahul's, her breath catching in her throat. The memories came flooding back—Darshan's voice, his smile, the way he had made her feel alive and terrified all at once.

Rahul noticed her reaction and squeezed her hand gently. "Are you okay?"

Kalpana forced herself to nod, but the truth was, she wasn't sure. The lines between past and present were blurring again, and she didn't know how to stop it.

"I just... I need some time," she said, pulling her hand away and standing up. "I think I should go."

Rahul looked concerned, but he didn't press her. "Do you want me to walk you back?"

"No, it's fine. I'll be okay." Kalpana tried to smile, but it felt hollow. "Thanks, Rahul. For everything."

He nodded, watching her with a mix of understanding and worry. "Anytime, Kalpana. Take care."

As Kalpana walked away, the music from the shack continued to play, the melody weaving itself into her thoughts, into the very fabric of her being. She knew she couldn't keep running from her past forever, but she also knew she wasn't ready to face it—not yet.

For now, all she could do was keep moving forward, one step at a time, even as the shadows of the music followed her, a constant reminder of the love she had lost and the life she was still trying to rebuild.

TEN
WAVES OF CONFESSION

The days after Kalpana's emotional evening on the beach with Rahul passed in a whirlwind of study sessions and late-night walks. Despite the turmoil she still felt, Rahul had a calming effect on her, anchoring her in the present even as the shadows of the past loomed large. They continued to meet, sometimes at the beach, sometimes at a small café tucked away in one of Goa's narrow lanes, where they would talk about everything and nothing.

Kalpana found herself looking forward to these moments more and more. Rahul's presence made her feel alive, and his unassuming nature allowed her to let her guard down in a way she hadn't been able to with anyone else. But even as their bond deepened, Kalpana couldn't shake the fear that her past would come back to haunt her, that she would lose herself in the illusion of Darshan again.

One evening, as they sat on the beach watching the sun dip below the horizon, Kalpana finally found the courage to confront her feelings.

"Rahul," she began, her voice hesitant, "there's something I need to tell you."

Rahul turned to her, his expression open and attentive. "What is it?"

Kalpana took a deep breath, the words she had been rehearsing for days suddenly seeming inadequate. "I've been carrying this around for a long time, and I think it's time I let it out. I—"

She faltered, the memories of Darshan flooding her mind. But then she looked at Rahul, saw the kindness in his eyes, and something inside her steadied.

"I think I'm falling in love with you," she said, her voice trembling. "I know it sounds crazy, and I know we've only known each other for a short time, but... it feels right."

For a moment, there was silence. The only sound was the gentle lapping of the waves against the shore. Kalpana's heart pounded in her chest, and she wondered if she had made a terrible mistake.

But then Rahul reached out and took her hand, his touch warm and reassuring. "Kalpana, I... I feel the same way," he said softly. "I've been trying to figure out how to tell you, but I didn't want to push you, especially knowing what you've been through."

Kalpana felt a rush of relief, her heart swelling with a mix of joy and disbelief. "You mean it?"

Rahul nodded, a smile spreading across his face. "I do. You're different, Kalpana. There's something about you that I can't quite put into words, but I know I want to be with you, to help you through whatever you're facing."

Tears welled up in Kalpana's eyes, but this time, they were tears of happiness. She had been so afraid to open up, to allow herself to feel something real after all the pain she had endured. But with Rahul, it felt different. It felt safe.

They sat together in silence for a while, their hands intertwined, the connection between them growing stronger with each passing moment. The worries that had plagued Kalpana's mind seemed to melt away, replaced by a sense of calm she hadn't felt in years.

As the evening deepened, they strolled along the beach, talking about their dreams and hopes for the future. Rahul confided in Kalpana about his passion for music, how he had always dreamed of becoming a professional singer but had never quite had the courage to pursue it fully.

"You should go for it," Kalpana said, her voice filled with conviction. "You have a gift, Rahul. Don't let it go to waste."

Rahul smiled, her words giving him a renewed sense of purpose. "And what about you? What are your dreams, Kalpana?"

Kalpana thought for a moment, her gaze drifting to the horizon. "I want to finish my MBA, to do something meaningful with my life. But more than that, I want to find peace, to move past everything that's happened and build a life that's truly mine."

"You will," Rahul said, his voice gentle but firm. "And I'll be right here, cheering you on."

In the days that followed, Kalpana and Rahul grew even closer. They spent their mornings studying together, with Rahul helping Kalpana stay focused on her assignments and exam preparations. His presence was like a balm to her frayed nerves, keeping her grounded even as the pressure of her studies mounted.

In turn, Kalpana became Rahul's biggest supporter, encouraging him to pursue his music with the same dedication she applied to her studies. She would listen to him practice, offering feedback and cheering him on as he worked on new songs. With her by his side, Rahul felt more confident than ever before, ready to chase the dreams he had once thought were out of reach.

They made a habit of spending their evenings at the beach, where they would talk, laugh, and share their thoughts on everything from the future to the small moments that made each day special. For Kalpana, these moments were like a lifeline, pulling her further and further away from the darkness of her past.

One evening, as they sat on the sand watching the stars come out, Rahul turned to Kalpana with a serious expression.

"Kalpana, I've been thinking," he began, his tone thoughtful. "We're both working so hard towards our goals, but I don't want us to lose sight of what's really important."

Kalpana looked at him, intrigued. "What do you mean?"

"I mean that no matter how busy we get, we need to remember to make time for each other, to keep supporting each other the way we are now," Rahul explained. "Because that's what makes everything worth it."

Kalpana smiled, her heart swelling with affection for him. "I couldn't agree more. No matter what happens, we'll face it together."

As they sat there, wrapped in the warmth of each other's presence, Kalpana felt something she hadn't felt in a long time: hope. Hope that she could build a future with Rahul, that she could overcome her past and create a life that was truly her own.

For the first time in years, Kalpana felt like she was on the right path, with someone by her side who understood her, supported her, and believed in her. And as they walked back along the beach that night, hand in hand, she knew that no matter what challenges lay ahead, she wouldn't have to face them alone.

ELEVEN

WHISPERS OF THE HEART

Kalpana's life had taken on a new rhythm, one filled with purpose and contentment. Her days were balanced between her rigorous MBA studies and the quiet joy she found in her relationship with Rahul. They were inseparable, supporting each other's dreams and providing the solace that both had longed for.

But as the end of the semester approached, bringing with it the mounting pressure of final exams and project deadlines, Kalpana began to feel the familiar stirrings of anxiety. The memories of her past failures, the breakdowns, and the overwhelming sense of not being able to cope crept back into her mind, threatening to unravel the peace she had worked so hard to build.

One evening, as she sat in her room poring over notes for an upcoming exam, the weight of it all became too much. She pushed her books aside, her heart racing, as thoughts of Darshan began to surface. Despite all her efforts to move on, the shadow of Darshan loomed over her, a constant reminder of the person she used to be—the person she feared she might still be.

Kalpana took a deep breath, trying to steady herself. "This isn't real," she whispered, pressing her hands to her temples. "Darshan isn't real."

But the more she tried to push the thoughts away, the more they seemed to take hold. She could almost hear his voice, could almost see him standing there, just out of reach. The lines between reality and illusion blurred, and for a moment, Kalpana felt as if she were teetering on the edge of the same abyss, she had fallen into all those years ago.

In desperation, she picked up her phone and called Rahul. His voice was a lifeline, pulling her back from the brink.

"Kalpana, what's wrong?" he asked, his concern evident.

"I... I'm scared, Rahul," she admitted, her voice trembling. "I feel like I'm losing control again, like everything is slipping away."

"Hey, it's okay," Rahul said gently. "Take a deep breath. I'm here with you."

His calm, steady tone helped to soothe the panic that had been building inside her. Kalpana closed her eyes, focusing on his voice, allowing it to anchor her in the present.

"Remember what you've accomplished, how far you've come," Rahul continued. "You're stronger than you think, Kalpana. You've faced these demons before, and you came out on the other side. You'll do it again."

Kalpana nodded, even though he couldn't see her. "You're right," she said, though her voice was still shaky. "I just... I don't want to go back to that place."

"And you won't," Rahul assured her. "You've got me, and you've got yourself. You're not alone in this."

After they hung up, Kalpana sat for a long time in the quiet of her room, letting his words sink in. She knew she had to face these fears head-on, to confront the part of her that was still trapped in the past. But she also knew that she didn't have to do it alone.

The next day, Rahul surprised Kalpana by taking her to a small, secluded part of the beach where they had never been before. It was a quiet spot, far from the usual crowds, where the only sound was the gentle rhythm of the waves.

"I thought we could both use a break," Rahul said with a smile as they sat down on the sand.

Kalpana smiled back, feeling the tension begin to ease from her shoulders. "You're right. This is perfect."

As they settled down, Rahul took out his phone, his eyes sparkling with mischief. "Let's capture this moment," he suggested, holding up the phone for a selfie.

Kalpana laughed, leaning into him as they both smiled for the camera. They took several pictures, some with serious poses, others with silly faces, their laughter echoing across the beach.

After a few more snaps, Rahul put his phone away and turned to Kalpana with a teasing grin. "So, any requests?"

Kalpana laughed, the sound light and free. "Surprise me."

Rahul began to play a soft, soulful melody, his voice blending with the sound of the waves. Kalpana closed her eyes, letting the music wash over her. But as the song continued, she felt a strange sense of déjà vu. The melody, the voice—it all seemed so familiar, so much like Darshan's.

She opened her eyes, and for a moment, she could almost see him there, in Rahul's place. The illusion was so strong that it made her heart skip a beat. But then, she blinked, and the image was gone. It was just Rahul, looking at her with that same gentle expression.

"Kalpana?" he asked, his voice filled with concern. "Are you okay?"

Kalpana hesitated, the words catching in her throat. "I... I'm fine," she managed to say, though the truth was far from it. The memories of Darshan were closer than ever, and she didn't know how to escape them.

As the days passed, Kalpana threw herself into her studies, trying to drown out the thoughts that plagued her. She spent long hours in the library, working on her final projects, trying to push past the fear and anxiety that threatened to consume her.

But no matter how hard she tried, she couldn't shake the feeling that Darshan was still with her, a ghost she couldn't escape. And as the pressure of her exams mounted, the lines between reality and illusion began to blur once more.

One evening, after a particularly exhausting day of studying, Kalpana decided to take a walk along the beach to clear her mind. She hadn't been sleeping well, and the weight of everything was beginning to take its toll.

As she walked, the sound of the waves seemed to echo the turmoil in her mind. She felt lost, adrift in a sea of memories and emotions she couldn't control.

And then, out of the corner of her eye, she saw him.

At first, she thought she was imagining it. But when she looked again, there he was, standing at the water's edge, his back to her. Darshan.

Kalpana's heart pounded in her chest as she took a hesitant step forward. "Darshan?" she called out, her voice trembling.

The figure didn't move, didn't respond. But Kalpana was certain it was him. She took another step, and then another, her breath coming in shallow gasps.

"Darshan!" she called out again, louder this time.

But as she got closer, the figure began to fade, dissolving into the mist and the waves. Kalpana's heart dropped, a wave of despair crashing over her.

"No, please," she whispered, tears streaming down her face. "Don't leave me again."

But he was gone, as if he had never been there at all.

Kalpana sank to her knees on the sand, her body wracked with sobs. She didn't know how long she sat there, crying out all the pain and fear she had been holding inside. When she finally looked up, the beach was empty, the only sound the gentle lapping of the waves against the shore.

Kalpana wiped her tears, taking a deep, shuddering breath. She knew now that she couldn't keep running from the past, couldn't keep pretending that Darshan didn't exist. He was a part of her, a part she needed to confront if she ever wanted to move forward.

As she made her way back to her room, Kalpana felt a sense of resolve begin to form within her. She didn't know what the future held, but she knew one thing for certain: she couldn't let Darshan control her life any longer.

She would face him, face herself, and find a way to break free from the shadows of the past.

And with Rahul by her side, she knew she had the strength to do it.

TWELVE

FRACTURED REALITY

Kalpana's days in Goa had become a blend of the present and echoes from the past. Though Rahul's presence in her life brought her comfort, there was always an undercurrent of unease—a feeling she couldn't quite shake. The closer she grew to Rahul, the more she was haunted by the memories of Darshan, and the fear that her mind might betray her again.

The upcoming final exams only added to her anxiety. The pressure to excel, coupled with the lingering trauma from her past, created a storm inside her that she struggled to control. As the days passed, the lines between reality and her imagination began to blur once more.

One evening, after a particularly grueling study session, Kalpana decided to take a break and call Rahul. She needed to hear his voice, to ground herself in something real.

"Hey, you," Rahul answered cheerfully, his voice instantly calming her frayed nerves. "How's the studying going?"

"It's... going," Kalpana replied, trying to keep her tone light. "I just needed a break. My mind feels like it's going to explode."

Rahul chuckled softly. "That's why you need to take it easy sometimes. Remember, it's just an exam. You're more important than any grade."

Kalpana smiled, though the weight of her thoughts made it difficult to fully enjoy the moment. "Thanks, Rahul. You always know just what to say."

"That's what I'm here for," he replied warmly. "How about we go for a walk on the beach tomorrow morning? Clear your head before the final stretch?"

"I'd love that," Kalpana said, genuinely looking forward to the idea. "Let's do it."

The next morning, Kalpana met Rahul on the beach as planned. The sun was just beginning to rise, casting a soft golden light over the water. They walked side by side, the sound of the waves a soothing backdrop to their conversation.

For a while, they talked about mundane things—Rahul's music, Kalpana's upcoming exams—but there was an unspoken tension between them, something that neither wanted to address.

After a while, Rahul stopped and turned to Kalpana, his expression serious. "Kalpana, there's something I need to ask you."

Kalpana's heart skipped a beat. "What is it?"

"You've been distant lately," Rahul said gently. "I can tell something's bothering you. Is it just the exams, or is there something more?"

Kalpana looked away, her gaze fixed on the horizon. She knew this moment would come, but she wasn't sure she was ready to face it.

"It's not just the exams," she admitted, her voice barely above a whisper. "It's everything... my past, the things I've been through... Darshan."

The name hung in the air between them, heavy and charged with emotion. Rahul's expression softened, and he took a step closer to her.

"You don't have to talk about it if you're not ready," he said, his voice full of understanding.

"No, I need to," Kalpana replied, finally meeting his eyes. "You deserve to know the truth."

Slowly, Kalpana began to recount her past—how she had fallen for Darshan, the way he had disappeared, and the devastating realization that he had never existed. She told Rahul about the breakdown that had followed, the years of therapy, and the fear that she might never fully recover.

Rahul listened intently, his expression a mix of concern and compassion. When she finished, he reached out and took her hand, his grip warm and reassuring.

"Kalpana," he said softly, "I'm so sorry you went through all of that. But I want you to know that you're not alone anymore. I'm here with you, and I'm not going anywhere."

Tears welled up in Kalpana's eyes, but this time they were tears of relief. She had been carrying this burden for so long, and now, finally, she could share it with someone who cared.

"Thank you, Rahul," she whispered, squeezing his hand. "I don't know what I'd do without you."

"You don't have to worry about that," Rahul said with a smile. "We'll get through this together."

They continued their walk, the tension between them eased by their conversation. But as they walked, Kalpana couldn't shake the feeling that something was still not right. The memories of Darshan were too vivid, too real, and she couldn't help but wonder if her mind was playing tricks on her again.

Later that day, as Kalpana sat alone in her room, she found herself scrolling through her old photos, searching for any evidence that Darshan had existed. But no matter how hard she looked, there was nothing—just empty memories and a growing sense of unease.

The following week, as she prepared for her final exams, Kalpana's anxiety reached a fever pitch. She was terrified of failing, not just academically, but mentally. The pressure to succeed, coupled with her unresolved trauma, was pushing her to the brink.

On the night before her first exam, Kalpana received a message from Rahul. It was a photo of the two of them on the beach, smiling and carefree. Below it, he had written: "Remember, you're stronger than you think. You've got this."

Kalpana stared at the message, her heart swelling with emotion. Rahul's unwavering support meant everything to her, but it also reminded her of the fragility of her own mind.

The next day, Kalpana sat in the exam hall, her heart pounding in her chest. As she looked down at the paper in front of her, her vision blurred, and for a moment, she felt like she was back at HMS College, sitting next to Darshan.

Panic gripped her, and she struggled to breathe. The walls seemed to close in around her, the noise of the other students fading into a distant hum.

But then, she remembered Rahul's words: "You're stronger than you think."

Kalpana closed her eyes, taking a deep breath. She wasn't that scared, broken girl anymore. She was someone who had faced her demons and survived. She could do this.

When she opened her eyes again, the panic had subsided, replaced by a steely resolve. She picked up her pen and began to write, her hand steady and sure.

As the exam progressed, Kalpana found herself falling into a rhythm, her confidence growing with each answer she wrote. By the time she finished, she felt a sense of accomplishment she hadn't felt in years.

As she walked out of the exam hall, the sun shining brightly overhead, Kalpana felt a weight lift from her shoulders. She had faced her fears and won, and she knew now that she could face whatever came next.

But as she looked out at the sea of students, her eyes caught a familiar figure in the crowd. For a split second, she thought she saw Darshan, standing there, watching her.

Kalpana blinked, and the figure was gone. Just a trick of the light, she told herself. But deep down, she knew that Darshan was still with her, a part of her that she might never fully escape.

As she walked away, Kalpana couldn't shake the feeling that the past wasn't finished with her yet. But for now, she would focus on the present, on the life she was building with Rahul, and on the future that awaited her.

The shadows of the past might still linger, but Kalpana was determined to keep moving forward, one step at a time.

THIRTEEN

FADING ECHOES

The days following the exams should have been a time of relief and celebration for Kalpana. Her academic journey was finally complete, and she was eager to spend more time with Rahul, the man who had brought warmth and joy back into her life. But as the days slipped by, Kalpana found herself gripped by an unsettling sense of dread.

It started with a missed call. Kalpana had been sitting in her hostel room, idly scrolling through her phone, when she noticed that Rahul hadn't returned her call. At first, she dismissed it, thinking he might be busy with his music. But as hours turned into days and her messages went unanswered, her anxiety grew.

She tried calling again, but his phone was unreachable. The message she had sent in the morning still showed a single tick—delivered but not read. The silence was suffocating, each moment stretching into an eternity as she waited for some sign, any sign, from Rahul.

By the third day, Kalpana couldn't take it anymore. The uncertainty was eating away at her, and she decided to visit the shack where Rahul usually performed. She hoped to find him there, strumming his guitar, ready with a reassuring smile to dispel all her fears.

But when she arrived at the shack, her heart sank. The place was alive with music and chatter, but Rahul was nowhere to be seen. Instead, a young man she didn't recognize was on stage, playing a familiar tune. Kalpana's heart raced as she made her way to the shack manager, a knot of dread tightening in her stomach.

"Where's Rahul?" she asked, trying to keep her voice steady.

The manager looked at her with mild confusion. "Rahul? He's right there," he said, nodding toward the man on stage.

Kalpana stared at the performer, her mind reeling. "No, not him. I mean the other Rahul. The one who used to sing here with his guitar."

The manager's brow furrowed as he tried to make sense of her words. "There's no other Rahul. This is the only Rahul we've had, and he's been performing here for the last two years."

Kalpana's heart plummeted. "No, you don't understand. The Rahul I know—he's different. He's..."

But as she trailed off, the manager's expression remained unchanged, a mix of sympathy and puzzlement. "I'm sorry, but there's only one Rahul here, and he's been with us for two years. Maybe you're mistaking him for someone else?"

The reality of the situation began to crash down on her. Kalpana felt her world tilt as she struggled to grasp what was happening. It couldn't be true. The Rahul she knew was real—she had talked to him, laughed with him, loved him. He couldn't just be...imaginary.

In a desperate attempt to prove herself right, Kalpana pulled out her phone. She hurriedly scrolled through her photos, her hands trembling as she found the selfies they had taken at the beach. But as she stared at the images, her heart froze.

In every photo, she was alone.

The selfies that had once brought her joy now filled her with a deep sense of dread. Rahul was nowhere to be seen. It was just her, smiling at the camera, the beach stretching out behind her, empty except for the waves crashing against the shore. The truth was undeniable.

Tears welled up in her eyes as she realized the full extent of her delusion. She had fallen in love with an illusion, and now, once again, she was left alone to pick up the shattered pieces of her heart.

Kalpana left the shack with her heart pounding, the manager's words echoing in her mind. As she stepped into the cab, she leaned back, closing her eyes in an attempt to escape the whirlwind of emotions threatening to engulf her. All she could hear was the sound of the waves crashing against the rocks—a relentless, unforgiving rhythm that mirrored the turmoil inside her. The waves, once a source of calm, now felt like a metaphor for her mental state—unpredictable, violent, and unyielding.

The ride back to her hostel felt interminable. Every bump in the road sent a fresh wave of doubt and despair washing over her. How could she have been so blind, so foolish? The world she had built around Rahul, the love she thought was real, had crumbled to dust in an instant. The weight of her loneliness pressed down on her, as inescapable as the ocean tides she could still hear in her mind.

When she finally reached her room, Kalpana sank onto her bed, her body heavy with exhaustion. The silence was deafening, a stark contrast to the noise in her head. For a few moments, she simply lay there, staring up at the ceiling, unable to move, unable to think. It was as if her mind had shut down, a defence mechanism against the overwhelming pain.

After a few days of living in this fog of despair, Kalpana reached out to her only friend in Goa—Meera. But when she dialled Meera's number, hoping to hear a comforting voice, she was met with disappointment. Meera was on vacation in Kerala, blissfully unaware of the storm raging in Kalpana's life. The realization that she was truly alone in Goa hit her like a punch to the gut.

With no one left to turn to, Kalpana made the difficult decision to leave. She packed her bags in a daze, her movements mechanical as she prepared to return home. The vibrant memories she had hoped to make in Goa had turned into a nightmare she was desperate to escape.

On the train, as Kalpana gazed out the window, the familiar sights of Goa began to fade away, just like the dreams she had once nurtured. Her eyes, filled with unshed tears, blurred the passing scenery until everything was a haze of green and blue. She couldn't hold back any longer—the tears spilled over, silently tracing paths down her cheeks.

Kalpana blamed herself for everything. For believing in Darshan, for falling for Rahul, for getting lost in a world of illusions she had created to escape her reality. The pain of her self-betrayal was the deepest cut of all. As she closed her eyes, the vibrant world outside faded to black, just as her dreams of being with Rahul had vanished into the void.

The rhythmic clatter of the train on the tracks was the only sound she could hear now, a distant echo of the life she was leaving behind. Kalpana knew that when she opened her eyes again, she would be far from Goa, far from the memories that now haunted her. But for now, she allowed herself to drift into that darkness, hoping that, somehow, she would find the strength to face the light again

THROUGH THE EYES OF PAIN

The train ride to Udupi was suffocating. Kalpana sat by the window, staring at the passing scenery, but all she could see was Rahul's face, his voice echoing in her mind. Her love for him had been real, tangible in a way that made everything else seem like a blur. She had believed in them, in their future together, in the way he had made her feel alive. But now, all that was left was a void—a gaping chasm where her heart used to be.

As the train rumbled on, tears slipped down her cheeks, silent but steady. The more she tried to push the thoughts away, the more they consumed her. Rahul was gone, just like Darshan had vanished before him, but this time it felt different. This time, it wasn't just about the mystery of his existence; it was about the love she had poured into something that was now nothing. The pain was unbearable, twisting inside her like a knife.

When the train finally pulled into Udupi, Kalpana felt numb. Her parents were there, waiting with anxious faces, but she barely registered their presence. She was like a ghost of her former self, drifting through the motions as they guided her home. They didn't bombard her with questions, sensing the fragility of her state. Instead, they offered their support in the quietest of ways—a comforting hand on her shoulder, a warm meal left at her bedside.

Kalpana retreated to her childhood bedroom, the walls now closing in on her like a cage. Memories of her time with Rahul played on a loop in her mind—his smile, his laughter, the way he had looked at her like she was the only one who mattered. She had given her heart to him, and now it lay shattered at her feet, the pieces too sharp to pick up.

Her parents watched her with heavy hearts, knowing that this pain was deeper than anything she had experienced before. They had seen her broken once by Darshan's disappearance, and now they were witnessing the fallout of a second, even more devastating blow. Desperate to help, they reached out to the old doctor who had treated Kalpana during her first breakdown, hoping he could guide them through this nightmare once more.

The doctor, a kind and wise man, remembered Kalpana well. He knew the fragility of her mind, the way it clung to the idea of love as a lifeline in a world that often felt overwhelming. He advised her parents to be patient, to give her time to grieve but to also encourage her to find a new purpose. "She needs to feel like she's moving forward," he said gently. "Help her see that life still has meaning, that there are still goals worth striving for."

Kalpana's parents took his advice to heart. They didn't push her to talk about Rahul or what had happened in Goa. Instead, they focused on helping her rebuild her life, bit by bit. They encouraged her to channel her pain into something productive, to turn her attention to her studies and career. They knew she had always been ambitious, driven by a desire to succeed, and they hoped that reigniting that fire would help her heal.

Slowly, Kalpana began to respond. The pain was still there, a constant ache that throbbed with every heartbeat, but she started to see a way through it. Her parents' unwavering support was like a balm to her wounded soul, and she clung to their encouragement like a lifeline. They reminded her of her strength, of all she had accomplished despite the obstacles thrown her way. And gradually, Kalpana began to believe them.

As the weeks turned into months, Kalpana started to feel the faintest glimmer of hope. The pain hadn't disappeared—it was still there, lingering beneath the surface—but it no longer consumed her every thought. She could see a future again, one that wasn't defined by her love for Rahul or the mystery of Darshan. It was a future she was building for herself, brick by brick, with the support of those who loved her.

And as she stood at the threshold of that future, Kalpana realized that she wasn't the same person who had fallen in love with Darshan, or even with Rahul. She was stronger now, forged in the fire of her pain and emerging with a new sense of purpose. She wasn't sure what lay ahead, but for the first time in a long while, she felt ready to face it.

FIFTEEN

SHADOWS OF DOUBT

Kalpana had always believed that completing her MBA would mark the beginning of a new chapter in her life, one where she could finally leave the pain of the past behind. After everything she had been through, she was determined to move forward and carve out a successful career for herself. Morningstarr, a renowned MNC, seemed like the perfect place for that fresh start.

The opportunity to interview at Morningstarr had filled her with a renewed sense of purpose. It felt like the culmination of all her hard work, a chance to prove that she could rise above her past and achieve something meaningful. She knew that this could be her last shot at a fresh start, the final step in reclaiming her life and finding a sense of stability.

Kalpana arrived in Mumbai a week before the interview, giving herself time to adjust to the city's bustling energy and to prepare herself mentally. She stayed in a modest hotel room, spending her days revising her notes, practicing potential interview questions, and visualizing her success.

She pushed aside the memories of Rahul and Darshan, focusing solely on the future she wanted to build.

The day of the interview arrived, and Kalpana walked into the towering Morningstarr building with a mixture of nerves and determination. The interview panel was composed of seasoned professionals, their questions probing and challenging. Kalpana had prepared for this, but as the interview progressed, she began to feel a creeping doubt. She stumbled over a few answers, hesitated when she should have been assertive, and missed opportunities to highlight her strengths.

As she left the interview room, Kalpana couldn't shake the feeling that she hadn't done enough. The self-assuredness she had carried with her into the building had evaporated, replaced by a gnawing uncertainty. She had pinned so much hope on this interview, convinced that this was her final opportunity to prove something in life. Now, as she walked back to her hotel, she was haunted by the thought that she had let it slip through her fingers.

Back in her room, Kalpana sat on the edge of the bed, her thoughts spiralling into a vortex of self-recrimination. She replayed the interview over and over in her mind, fixating on every mistake, every moment of hesitation. She had convinced herself that this was her last chance to move on from her past, to rebuild her life on her terms. But now, all she could feel was the crushing weight of disappointment.

The idea that she might have failed at Morningstarr was unbearable. This interview had been more than just a career opportunity—it had been a symbol of her determination to overcome the trauma of the past, to prove to herself that she was capable of success. But now, that dream felt fragile, slipping through her grasp like sand.

For days after the interview, Kalpana was plagued by doubt and anxiety. The haunting question of whether she had done enough gnawed at her, making it impossible to focus on anything else. She had always been her harshest critic, but this time, the stakes felt impossibly high. She had staked everything on this interview, believing it was her final shot at a fresh start. The thought of failing was more than she could bear.

Mumbai's vibrant energy, which had initially filled her with hope, now felt overwhelming. The city's noise and chaos mirrored the turmoil in her mind. As the days passed, Kalpana found it increasingly difficult to stay positive. The memories of Rahul and Darshan, of all the pain and confusion they had brought into her life, resurfaced, blending with her current fears and insecurities.

Despite the fear that gripped her, Kalpana knew she couldn't afford to give up. She had come too far, worked too hard, to let this setback define her. But the doubt lingered, casting a shadow over everything. She had wanted so desperately to prove something to herself, to move on from her past and build a successful future. But now, all she could do was wait and hope that her efforts had been enough.

As she sat in her hotel room, staring out at the city lights, Kalpana knew that the road ahead would not be easy. The interview at Morningstarr had shaken her confidence, but it hadn't broken her. She would continue to fight for her future, to rebuild her life, one step at a time. But the haunting fear of failure, of having missed her last chance, would stay with her, a reminder of just how much was at stake.

SIXTEEN

IN THE CROSSROADS

Kalpana had spent days anxiously waiting for news from Morningstarr, her heart racing each time her phone buzzed with a notification. The uncertainty gnawed at her, making it difficult to focus on anything else. Then, one morning, her phone rang, and the name "Morningstarr" flashed on the screen. Her pulse quickened as she answered the call, and the voice on the other end brought news she had been desperately hoping for—she had been selected for the final round.

The final round was to be a stress interview with key stakeholders. It was designed to test not just her knowledge and skills, but her ability to remain composed under pressure. Kalpana knew that this would be the ultimate test of her resilience and determination. She had to prove that she was capable of handling the challenges that came with the role. This was her moment, her chance to finally reclaim her life.

The day of the interview arrived, and Kalpana left her hotel with a mixture of nerves and determination. As her cab wove through Mumbai's chaotic traffic, she tried to steady her racing thoughts, mentally rehearsing her answers and strategies. She was determined to give her best, to push aside the doubts that had plagued her since her last interview.

But as the cab came to a halt in a traffic jam, something caught her eye. Among the swarm of street vendors weaving between the cars, a familiar figure appeared, selling car accessories to the drivers. Her breath caught in her throat as she recognized him—Darshan. He was moving from vehicle to vehicle, offering miniature guitar key chains to the drivers. The sight of him sent a shockwave through her, momentarily freezing her in place.

Darshan, or at least the person who looked like him, reached Kalpana's window. He smiled at her, holding up a bunch of key chains, and asked in Hindi, "Madam, key chain chahiye? (Madam, do you want a key chain?)"

For a split second, Kalpana's world tilted on its axis. Was this really Darshan? How could he be here, selling trinkets in the middle of Mumbai's traffic? Her mind raced, trying to make sense of what she was seeing. But before she could respond, the traffic began to move, and the cab pulled away, leaving Darshan—and her confusion—behind.

Kalpana's heart pounded in her chest as she struggled to process what had just happened. Was it really him? Or was this another figment of her imagination, a manifestation of the stress and anxiety she had been carrying? She knew she couldn't afford to dwell on it now, not with the most important interview of her life ahead of her. Closing her eyes, she forced herself to take deep breaths, trying to calm her racing thoughts. She had to focus, had to put everything she had into this interview.

Arriving at the Morningstarr office, Kalpana steeled herself for what was to come. The interview was one of the toughest she had ever faced. The questions were relentless, probing into her understanding of the business, her problem-solving skills, and her ability to stay composed under pressure. But despite the challenges, Kalpana responded with confidence, drawing on her years of experience and the resilience she had built through her struggles.

As the interview neared its conclusion, one of the panel members leaned forward, his expression unreadable. He gave her some initial feedback, acknowledging her strengths and pointing out areas for improvement. Then, he requested that she wait at the canteen on the top floor. One of their senior HRs was running late, and after they discussed her performance, the result would be sent to her phone.

Kalpana nodded, her heart still racing from the intensity of the interview. As she made her way to the canteen, she couldn't shake the image of Darshan from her mind. Was it really him, or had her mind played tricks on her again? She tried to push the thought aside, knowing that she needed to stay focused on the present. This interview was her chance to start anew, to finally put her past behind her.

Sitting in the canteen, Kalpana looked out at the sprawling cityscape of Mumbai. She knew that whatever happened next, she had given her best. All she could do now was wait, hoping that this time, the future would be kinder to her.

SEVENTEEN

ECHOES OF THE PAST

Kalpana sat in the canteen, the sprawling view of Mumbai stretching out before her. The city hummed with life, a relentless energy that mirrored the storm of thoughts swirling in her mind. She gripped her phone tightly, her knuckles white as she fought to steady her racing heart. As she stared out of the window, the memories began to flood in, unbidden and overwhelming.

She saw herself back in college, full of hopes and dreams, before everything began to unravel. Darshan's enigmatic presence, the strange connection she felt with him, and the haunting confusion that followed his sudden disappearance. Then Rahul, with his gentle voice and kind eyes, a beacon of light in her darkest moments, only to vanish just like Darshan had. It was still unbelievable, the way both of them had simply faded away, leaving her alone with the pain of lost love.

The weight of it all pressed down on her, the loneliness, the heartache, the endless questions that had no answers. Her eyes began to sting, and before she knew it, tears were welling up, blurring the chaotic cityscape into a watery mosaic of colours and lights.

Suddenly, her phone vibrated in her hand, jolting her back to the present. She wiped her tears hastily, trying to compose herself as she glanced down at the screen. But before she could even process the message, she heard the faint creak of the canteen door opening.

Her heart skipped a beat as she looked up, still blinking away the remnants of her tears. Through her blurred vision, she saw a tall, lean man dressed impeccably in a well-fitted formal suit, approaching her table with purposeful strides. He moved with a calm confidence that suggested he was someone important, someone with authority.

Kalpana's mind raced, assuming this must be the senior HR manager she was supposed to meet. She tried to steady her breathing, focusing on the fact that this was it—her moment of truth. The man sat down across from her, his expression warm and congratulatory.

"Congratulations, Kalpana. You've been selected for the role," he said, his voice smooth and reassuring.

For a moment, Kalpana couldn't respond. The words hung in the air, but their meaning seemed distant, overshadowed by the shock of recognition. She blinked, trying to make sense of what she was seeing. Sitting in front of her, congratulating her on her new job, was Rahul. The same Rahul who had disappeared without a trace, the one she had thought about endlessly, the one she had loved.

Her breath caught in her throat, and all the emotions she had been trying to suppress came rushing back, overwhelming her senses. The happiness of getting the job was momentarily forgotten, eclipsed by the sheer disbelief of seeing him here, now.

"Where were you?" The words tumbled out of her mouth before she could stop them, her voice shaky and filled with a mixture of relief, confusion, and lingering hurt.

Rahul looked at her with a soft, knowing smile, his eyes reflecting a depth of emotion that sent a shiver down her spine. "We are always with you, Kalpana," he said gently, his voice carrying a weight that seemed to resonate with something deep within her. "Always."

The simplicity of his words struck her, echoing in the quiet space between them. It was as if he was speaking to something beyond just the present moment, something that had always been a part of her journey, her struggles, and her growth. The room seemed to blur around them, leaving only the two of them, locked in a moment that felt both surreal and profoundly real.

Kalpana's mind raced to make sense of it all, but for the first time in a long time, she felt a sense of peace, a strange acceptance of the mysteries that had haunted her for so long. Perhaps it didn't matter where Rahul or Darshan had gone, or whether they were real or figments of her imagination. What mattered was that she had found herself through it all—her strength, her resilience, and her ability to keep moving forward, no matter how many times she had been knocked down.

As she sat there, staring into Rahul's familiar eyes, she felt the weight of the past begin to lift, replaced by a quiet resolve. She was ready for whatever came next, knowing that, in some way, she was never truly alone.

EIGHTEEN

THE FINAL REVELATION

Kalpana sat in stunned silence, her mind swirling with confusion and disbelief as she faced Rahul—or was it Darshan? She couldn't be sure anymore. The man in front of her, so familiar yet so distant, had just shattered her reality. "Do you remember any of your doctor visits after the Darshan incident?" he asked gently.

Kalpana searched her memory, but it was like trying to grasp smoke. Everything was hazy, fragmented. "No... I don't remember," she admitted, her voice barely above a whisper.

Rahul—or Darshan—nodded as if he expected her answer. "Try to remember your childhood," he urged. "Think of the times when you felt lost, when you were overwhelmed by the pressure to be perfect. What did you do to cope?"

Flashes of her childhood came rushing back—moments when she felt suffocated by her parents' expectations, times when she wished she could escape, be someone else, live a life free of academic pressure. Slowly, pieces of a puzzle began to fit together. Darshan and Rahul were never just figments of her imagination; they were manifestations of her deepest desires, her unfulfilled dreams, her alter egos.

Kalpana's hands trembled as she placed them on the table, staring at them as if they belonged to someone else. "You mean... all those things Darshan did... the singing, the carefree life... it was me?" she asked, her voice quivering with the realization.

Rahul—no, Darshan—smiled softly, a look of understanding in his eyes. "Yes, Kalpana. You did those things. Darshan was your escape, your way of living the life you were denied. And when he was gone, the pressure of your studies created Rahul, to console you, to love you when you couldn't love yourself."

Kalpana shook her head, refusing to believe it. "No, this is all a lie!" she cried out, shutting her eyes tightly as if to block out the truth. But when she opened them again, it was Darshan sitting in front of her, not Rahul. His presence felt like a final blow to her crumbling sense of reality.

"You were diagnosed with Dissociative Identity Disorder, Kalpana," Darshan said gently, his voice full of empathy. "You created us to cope with the pressures that were too much for you to bear alone."

Kalpana felt her world collapsing around her. The joy of landing the job, the excitement of starting a new chapter in her life—all of it faded into the background as the weight of this revelation crushed her. Unable to face it, she abruptly stood up, booked a cab, and fled the office.

As she sat in the back seat, rain began to pour down, the droplets racing down the window, mirroring the tears streaming down her face. She pulled out her phone, desperately searching through her photo gallery for proof—proof that Rahul was real, that their moments together weren't just figments of her fractured mind. For a fleeting moment, she thought she saw a picture of them together, but as quickly as it appeared, it was gone, leaving only images of herself, alone.

Staring at the raindrops, her tears mingled with the rain outside. It was then that she remembered—whenever she felt trapped, whenever the weight of her life became too much to bear, she created Darshan. He was the part of her that lived freely, did everything she couldn't. And when he was gone, Rahul emerged, a fragment of herself that soothed her pain, loved her when no one else could.

As the cab sped through the rain-soaked streets, Kalpana realized the heart-breaking truth: Darshan and Rahul were parts of her, and now they were gone. But would they return? Would she need them again? Only time would tell. For now, she was left to face the world on her own, with the knowledge that the greatest love and the greatest pain she had ever known were born from within her own mind.

Dissociative Identity Disorder (did) And Mental Health

Dissociative Identity Disorder (DID) is a complex psychological condition often rooted in trauma, particularly severe and chronic abuse experienced during childhood. DID is characterized by the presence of two or more distinct personality states or identities, each with its own pattern of perceiving and interacting with the world. These identities may have unique names, ages, genders, and even memories or behaviours.

While DID is relatively rare, affecting around 1% of the population globally, its impact on individuals is profound. In India, where mental health awareness is still in its nascent stages, the challenges for those living with DID can be overwhelming. Due to cultural stigmas, lack of understanding, and inadequate mental health infrastructure, individuals with DID often go undiagnosed or misdiagnosed, leading to years of untreated trauma and suffering.

Mental Health in India

India faces a significant mental health crisis, with over 200 million people reported to suffer from various mental health disorders. However, only a fraction of these individuals receives adequate treatment. The reasons for this gap are multifaceted: stigma associated with mental illness, lack of awareness, and limited access to mental health care professionals. DID, like many other mental health conditions, often goes unrecognized in the broader public discourse.

Recent studies indicate that India has a severe shortage of mental health professionals, with only about 0.3 psychiatrists per 100,000 people. This shortage exacerbates the struggles of those with DID, as they require specialized and often long-term therapeutic interventions.

The Importance of Mental Health Care and Support

Mental health is just as crucial as physical health, yet it remains a neglected area in many societies, including India. For individuals living with DID, the journey to healing is complex and requires a supportive environment. This includes access to qualified mental health professionals, support from family and friends, and societal acceptance and understanding.

Families and communities play a pivotal role in the recovery process. By fostering an environment of empathy and understanding, they can help individuals with DID feel safe and supported, which is essential for the therapeutic process. Mental health education should also be a priority, enabling people to recognize symptoms and seek timely help.

How to Support Someone with DID

Supporting someone with DID involves patience, understanding, and a non-judgmental attitude. It's essential to:

1. **Educate Yourself:** Understanding the basics of DID and its impact on an individual's life can help you offer better support.

1. **Be a Good Listener:** Allow the person to express themselves without interruption or judgment.
2. **Encourage Professional Help:** Gently suggest seeking help from a mental health professional and offer to assist them in finding resources.

4. **Maintain Consistency:** People with DID often crave

stability and consistency, so try to be a reliable presence in their lives.

5. **Respect Boundaries:** Understand that each identity within a person with DID has its own boundaries and respect them.

In Conclusion

The story you've just read is a fictional representation of the struggles faced by someone living with DID. However, the emotions, confusion, and pain portrayed are very real for many individuals battling this disorder in silence. As a society, we must recognize the importance of mental health and work towards creating a world where everyone feels safe to seek help without fear of stigma or discrimination.